The World's No. 1 S

ROALD DAHL'S

STORY-SKETCHER

ILLUSTRATED BY Quentin Blake

AND YOU!

Create! Doodle!

Imagine!

GROSSET & DUNLAP
Published by the Penguin Group
Penguin Group (USA) LLC, 375 Hudson Street, New York, New York 10014, USA

USA | Canada | UK | Ireland | Australia | New Zealand | India | South Africa | China

penguin.com
A Penguin Random House Company

ISBN 978-0-448-48160-9   10 9 8 7 6 5 4 3 2 1

THIS BOOK BELONGS TO

_____

THIS IS A FABULOUS BOOK FULL OF FABULOUS THINGS!

Inside these pages, you will find bits and bobs from Roald Dahl's whipple-scrumptious stories, together with slivers and slices of artwork by Quentin Blake. Use your noggin to fill in the blank parts and help complete the pictures with whatever skills you may have.

CHARLIE AND THE CHOCOLATE FACTORY: Charlie Bucket is a small, poor boy who lives with his two parents and four grandparents in a little wooden house with one big bed. The only thing that Charlie really, truly wants is chocolate. Chocolate, chocolate, chocolate! So when he finds the last Golden Ticket that will win him a trip to the mysterious chocolate factory owned by Willy Wonka, Charlie is the happiest small, poor boy alive. Charlie, along with four other (not-quite-so-nice) children, has a trip that he won't be forgetting anytime soon.

ESIO TROT: Mr. Hoppy is desperately, despairingly, hopelessly in love with Mrs. Silver. Mrs. Silver is desperately, despairingly, hopelessly in love with Alfie, her pet tortoise. So when she tells Mr. Hoppy that she wishes Alfie were a little bigger, Mr. Hoppy knows he will win her heart if he can help her. The situation seems hopeless, until he decides that a made-up magic spell will just have to do the trick.

JAMES AND THE GIANT PEACH: James Henry Trotter is a happy boy, until his parents are eaten by a rhinoceros, and he is sent to live with his rotten Aunt Spiker and vile Aunt Sponge, who live on top of a big hill that is nowhere near the seaside. Then, James becomes a miserable boy. That is, until a strange old man gives him some magical crystals that create one enormous peach! The peach is quite the source of excitement for Aunt Spiker and Aunt Sponge, but an even bigger source of excitement for James, for inside the peach, he finds some creatures to take him on the adventure of a lifetime.

MATILDA: Matilda is a brilliant young girl with horrid parents. Though Matilda loves to read books, her father thinks that books are filthy and useless things, and her mother barely knows what books are at all. Luckily for Matilda, she finds a delightful teacher named Miss Honey, who can see that Matilda is just wonderful. Unluckily for Matilda *and* Miss Honey, the school headmistress is a beastly woman named Miss Trunchbull, who spends her days terrorizing children and throwing things. Matilda and Miss Honey must work together to defeat the Trunchbull once and for all.

THE TWITS: Mr. Twit and Mrs. Twit are two revolting people who live in a house without windows on an overgrown piece of ground that contains nothing other than a cage of monkeys and a dead tree. The Twits hate other people, especially naughty little boys, and more especially each other. They spend their days making disgusting pies and playing mean tricks, until finally the monkeys decide to step in and deal with them!

CHARLIE AND THE GREAT GLASS ELEVATOR: After being given a chocolate factory (yes, a WHOLE factory!), Charlie Bucket takes a voyage into outer space in a flying glass elevator. Charlie, along with his two parents, his four grandparents, their one big bed, and of course Willy Wonka, fights Vermicious Knids and saves flabbergasted astronauts while trying to make his way back to visit the president. And that's when things really get started . . .

THE MAGIC FINGER: It's really not her fault; it's not that she *tries* to do it. She doesn't want to, but she simply can't control herself. When she gets angry or upset—very, *very* angry or upset—a power in her finger takes over. She closes her eyes, looks the other way, and . . . !

DANNY THE CHAMPION OF THE WORLD:
Danny loves living his quiet life with his father in an old gypsy caravan behind the filling station, even with the pompous Mr. Hazell driving by in his big, shiny car. But life becomes a bit less quiet when Danny hears about his father's secret and very sneaky nighttime hobby. Armed with some raisins, some glue, and a hat, Danny sets off to help his father pull off the greatest caper Mr. Hazell will ever see.

FANTASTIC MR. FOX: Mr. Fox and his family would be content living in their small burrow under a tree, if it weren't for three nasty farmers: Boggis, Bunce, and Bean. The farmers are fed up with Mr. Fox stealing their livestock, so they decide to rid their farms of the foxes once and for all! What they don't reckon on is that Mr. Fox is a very clever fox indeed, and is not going to be giving up in a hurry.

GEORGE'S MARVELOUS MEDICINE: George is a very sweet boy. Really, truly, he is. It's just unfortunate that he has a very nasty grandmother who bosses him around and orders him to bring her medicine. George has no choice but to make sure her medicine will really, truly cure her—of her nastiness (and perhaps get rid of that smell, too). George puts everything he can find into his marvelous medicine, but the results don't end up being quite what he expected.

CHARLIE BUCKET'S FAMILY

"The whole of this family– the six grownups (count them) and little Charlie Bucket–live together in a small wooden house on the edge of a great town.

The house wasn't nearly large enough for so many people, and life was extremely uncomfortable for them all. There were only two rooms in the place altogether, and there was only one bed. The bed was given to the four old grandparents because they were so old and tired. They were so tired, they never got out of it.

Grandpa Joe and Grandma Josephine on this side, Grandpa George and Grandma Georgina on this side.

In the evenings, after he had finished his supper of watery cabbage soup, Charlie always went into the room of his four grandparents to listen to their stories, and then afterwards to say good night.

Every one of these old people was over ninety. They were as shriveled as prunes, and as bony as skeletons, and throughout the day, until Charlie made his appearance, they lay huddled in their one bed, two at either end, with nightcaps on to keep their heads warm, dozing the time away with nothing to do. But as soon as they heard the door opening, and heard Charlie's voice saying, "Good evening, Grandpa Joe and Grandma Josephine, and Grandpa George and Grandma Georgina," then all four of them would suddenly sit up, and their old wrinkled faces would light up with smiles of pleasure–and the talking would begin. For they loved this little boy. He was the only bright thing in their lives, and his evening visits were something that they looked forward to all day long. Often, Charlie's mother and father would come in as well, and stand by the door, listening to the stories that the old people told; and thus, for perhaps half an hour every night, this room would become a happy place, and the whole family would forget that it was hungry and poor."

Four old people in *one* big bed?! Draw Grandpa Joe and Grandma Josephine on one side of the bed, and Grandpa George and Grandma Georgina on the other side of the bed. Is there any space left for Charlie?

The Golden Tickets

"I, Willy Wonka, have decided to allow five children–just *five*, mind you, and no more–to visit my factory this year. These lucky five will be shown around personally by me, and they will be allowed to see all the secrets and the magic of my factory. Then, at the end of the tour, as a special present, all of them will be given enough chocolates and candies to last them for the rest of their lives! So watch out for the Golden Tickets! Five Golden Tickets have been printed on golden paper, and these five Golden Tickets have been hidden underneath the ordinary wrapping paper of five ordinary candy bars. These five candy bars may be anywhere–in any shop in any street in any town in any country in the world–upon any counter where Wonka's candies are sold. And the five lucky finders of these five Golden Tickets are the *only* ones who will be allowed to visit my factory and see what it's like *now* inside! Good luck to you all, and happy hunting! (Signed, Willy Wonka.)"

Nothing could be ever so great as winning a Golden Ticket! What do you think the Golden Tickets look like? Draw the shiny paper wrapped around a chocolate bar below.

FOUR TICKETS FOUND

"The very next day the first Golden Ticket was found.

The finder was a boy called Augustus Gloop, and Mr. Bucket's evening newspaper carried a large picture of him on the front page. The picture showed a nine-year-old boy who was so enormously fat he looked as though he had been blown up with a powerful pump. Great flabby folds of fat bulged out from every part of his body, and his face was like a monstrous ball of dough with two small greedy curranty eyes peering out upon the world.

✳ ✳ ✳

Suddenly, on the day before Charlie Bucket's birthday, the newspapers announced that the second Golden Ticket had been found. The lucky person was a small girl called Veruca Salt who lived with her rich parents in a great city far away. Once again, Mr. Bucket's evening newspaper carried a big picture of the finder. She was sitting between her beaming father and mother in the living room of their house, waving the Golden Ticket above her head, and grinning from ear to ear.

✳ ✳ ✳

"The third ticket," read Mr. Bucket, holding the newspaper up close to his face because his eyes were bad and he couldn't afford glasses, "the third Ticket was found by a Miss Violet Beauregarde. There was great excitement in the Beauregarde household when our reporter arrived to interview the lucky young lady–cameras were clicking and flashbulbs were flashing and people were pushing and jostling and trying to get a bit closer to the famous girl. And the famous girl was standing on a chair in the living room waving the Golden Ticket madly at arm's length as though she were flagging a taxi. She was talking very fast and very loudly to everyone, but it was not easy to hear all that she said because she was chewing so ferociously upon a piece of gum at the same time."

✳ ✳ ✳

"And who got the fourth Golden Ticket, Daddy?" Charlie asked.

"Now, let me see," said Mr. Bucket, peering at the newspaper again. "Ah yes, here we are. The fourth Golden Ticket," he read, "was found by a boy called Mike Teavee."

"Another bad lot, I'll be bound," muttered Grandma Josephine.

"Don't interrupt, Grandma," said Mrs. Bucket.

"The Teavee household," said Mr. Bucket, going on with his reading, "was crammed, like all the others, with excited visitors when our reporter arrived, but young Mike Teavee, the lucky winner, seemed extremely annoyed by the whole business. 'Can't you fools see I'm watching television?' he said angrily, 'I wish you wouldn't interrupt!'

"The nine-year-old boy was seated before an enormous television set, with his eyes glued to the screen, and he was watching a film in which one bunch of gangsters was shooting up another bunch of gangsters with machine guns. Mike Teavee himself had no less than eighteen toy pistols of various sizes hanging from belts around his body, and every now and again he would leap up into the air and fire off half a dozen rounds from one or another of these weapons."

Four not-so-nice young children have won four of the coveted Golden Tickets! It just doesn't seem fair to Charlie. In the spaces below, draw:

the big Augustus Gloop,

the spoiled Veruca Salt,

the gum-chewing Violet Beauregarde,

and the TV-watching Mike Teavee.

The Oompa-Loompas

"**T**he tiny men—they were no larger than medium-sized dolls—had stopped what they were doing, and now they were staring back across the river at the visitors. One of them pointed towards the children, and then he whispered something to the other four, and all five of them burst into peals of laughter.

"But they can't be *real* people," Charlie said.

"Of course they're real people," Mr. Wonka answered. "They're Oompa-Loompas. **"**

What would a *real* person from Loompaland look like? Draw some Oompa-Loompas in the space below. Try drawing them all in different poses!

"Mr. Willy Wonka can make marshmallows that taste of violets, and rich caramels that change color every ten seconds as you suck them, and little feathery sweets that melt away deliciously the moment you put them between your lips. He can make chewing gum that never loses its taste, and candy balloons that you can blow up to enormous sizes before you pop them with a pin and gobble them up. And, by a most secret method, he can make lovely blue birds' eggs with black spots on them, and when you put one of these in your mouth, it gradually gets smaller and smaller until suddenly there is nothing left except a tiny little pink sugary baby bird sitting on the tip of your tongue."

Mr. Willy Wonka makes candy that is more delicious than you could even imagine. Draw some of his scrumdiddlyumptious candy inventions in the space below.

INSIDE THE CHOCOLATE ROOM

"An important room, this!" cried Mr. Wonka, taking a bunch of keys from his pocket and slipping one into the keyhole of the door. "*This* is the nerve center of the whole factory, the heart of the whole business! And so *beautiful*! I *insist* upon my rooms being beautiful! I can't *abide* ugliness in factories! *In* we go, then! But *do* be careful, my dear children!

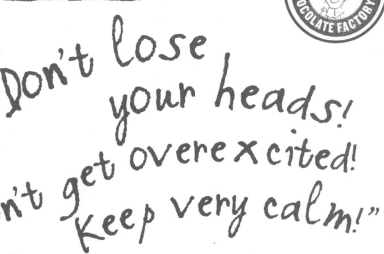

Don't lose your heads! Don't get overexcited! Keep very calm!"

Mr. Wonka opened the door. Five children and nine grownups pushed their ways in—and *oh*, what an amazing sight it was that now met their eyes!

They were looking down upon a lovely valley. There were green meadows on either side of the valley, and along the bottom of it there flowed a great brown river.

What is more, there was a tremendous waterfall halfway along the river—a steep cliff over which the water curled and rolled in a solid sheet, and then went crashing down into a boiling, churning whirlpool of froth and spray.

Below the waterfall (and this was the most astonishing sight of all), a whole mass of enormous glass pipes were dangling down into the river from somewhere high up in the ceiling! They really were *enormous*, those pipes. There must have been a dozen of them at least, and they were sucking up the brownish muddy water from the river and carrying it away to goodness knows where. And because they were made of glass, you could see the liquid flowing and bubbling along inside them, and above the noise of the waterfall, you could hear the never-ending suck-suck-sucking sound of the pipes as they did their work. **99**

Willy Wonka's Chocolate Room is all you could ever dream of! If you could make your very own Chocolate Room, what would it look like? Draw it here!

A Chocolate Waterfall

"The waterfall is *most* important!" Mr. Wonka went on. "It mixes the chocolate! It churns it up! It pounds it and beats it! It makes it light and frothy! No other factory in the world mixes its chocolate by waterfall! But it's the *only* way to do it properly! The *only* way!"

A waterfall made of *chocolate*? It must be the most delicious waterfall in the whole world! Can you draw the chocolate waterfall mixing and churning and pounding and beating the chocolate?

MR. HOPPY AND MRS. SILVER

"Mr. Hoppy lived in a small flat high up in a tall concrete building. He lived alone. He had always been a lonely man, and now that he was retired from work he was more lonely than ever.

There were two loves in Mr. Hoppy's life. One was the flowers he grew on his balcony. They grew in pots and tubs and baskets, and in summer the little balcony became a riot of color.

Mr. Hoppy's second love was a secret he kept entirely to himself.

The balcony immediately below Mr. Hoppy's jutted out a good bit further from the building than his own, so Mr. Hoppy always had a fine view of what was going on down there. This balcony belonged to an attractive middle-aged lady called Mrs. Silver. Mrs. Silver was a widow who also lived alone. And although she didn't know it, it was she who was the object of Mr. Hoppy's secret love. He had loved her from his balcony for many years, but he was a very shy man and he had never been able to bring himself to give her even the smallest hint of his love.

Every morning, Mr. Hoppy and Mrs. Silver exchanged polite conversation, the one looking down from above, the other looking up, but that was as far as it ever went. The distance between their balconies might not have been more than a few yards, but to Mr. Hoppy it seemed like a million miles. He longed to invite Mrs. Silver up for a cup of tea and a biscuit, but every time he was about to form the words on his lips, his courage failed him. As I said, he was a very very shy man.

Oh, if only, he kept telling himself, if only he could do something tremendous like saving her life or rescuing her from a gang of armed thugs, if only he could perform some great feat that would make him a hero in her eyes. If only . . .

The trouble with Mrs. Silver was that she gave all her love to somebody else, and that somebody was a small tortoise called Alfie. Every day when Mr. Hoppy looked over his balcony and saw Mrs. Silver whispering endearments to Alfie and stroking his shell, he felt absurdly jealous. He wouldn't even have minded becoming a tortoise himself if it meant Mrs. Silver stroking his shell each morning and whispering endearments to him. "

Poor Mr. Hoppy, ever so quietly in love with Mrs. Silver. Draw Mr. Hoppy standing on his balcony, surrounded by plants, and looking down at the wonderful Mrs. Silver on her balcony below.

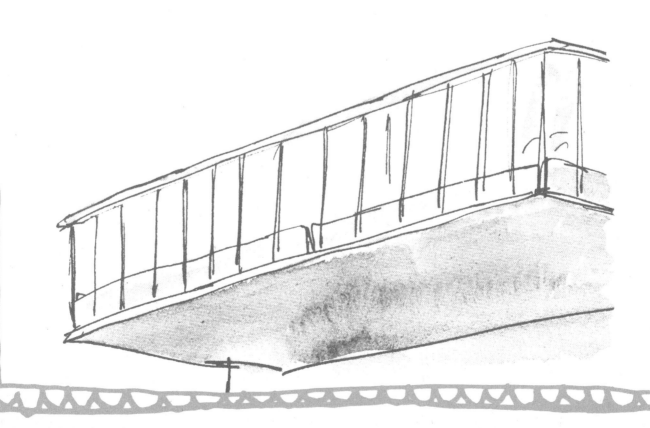

The Magic Words

"Mrs. Silver," he said. "I do actually happen to know how to make tortoises grow faster, if that's really what you want."

"You do?" she cried. "Oh, please tell me! Am I feeding him the wrong things?"

"I worked in North Africa once," Mr. Hoppy said. "That's where all these tortoises in England come from, and a bedouin tribesman told me the secret."

✳ ✳ ✳

In a couple of minutes Mr. Hoppy was back on the balcony with a sheet of paper in his hand. "I'm going to lower it to you on a bit of string," he said, "or it might blow away. Here it comes."

Mrs. Silver caught the paper and held it up in front of her. This is what she read:

ESIO TROT, ESIO TROT,
TEG REGGIB REGGIB!

EMOC NO, ESIO TROT,
WORG PU, FFUP PU, TOOHS PU!
GNIRPS PU, WOLB PU, LLEWS PU!
EGROG! ELZZUG! FFUTS! PLUG!
TUP NO TAF, ESIO TROT, TUP NO TAF!
TEG NO, TEG NO! ELBBOG DOOF!

"What *does* it mean?" she asked. "Is it another language?"

"It's tortoise language," Mr. Hoppy said. "Tortoises are very backward creatures. Therefore they can only understand words that are written backwards. That's obvious, isn't it?"

"I suppose so," Mrs. Silver said, bewildered.

"Esio trot is simply tortoise spelled backwards," Mr. Hoppy said. "Look at it."

"So it is," Mrs. Silver said.

"The other words are spelled backwards, too," Mr. Hoppy said. "If you turn them round into human language, they simply say . . . "

What do the words say in human language? Write the backwards words out forwards to see what the poem says.

ONE HUNDRED AND FORTY TORTOISES

"The only furniture in Mr. Hoppy's small living room was a table and two chairs. These he moved into his bedroom. Then he went out and bought a sheet of thick canvas and spread it over the entire living room floor to protect his carpet.

Next, he got out the telephone book and wrote down the address of every pet shop in the city. There were fourteen of them altogether.

It took him two days to visit each pet shop and choose his tortoises. He wanted a great many, at least one hundred, perhaps more. And he had to choose them very carefully.

To you and me there is not much difference between one tortoise and another. They differ only in their size and in the color of their shells. Alfie had a darkish shell, so Mr. Hoppy chose only the darker-shelled tortoises for his great collection.

Size, of course, was everything. Mr. Hoppy chose all sorts of different sizes, some weighing only slightly more than Alfie's thirteen ounces, others a great deal more, but he didn't want any that weighed less.

"Feed them cabbage leaves," the pet shop owners told him. "That's all they'll need. And a bowl of water."

✳ ✳ ✳

When he had finished, Mr. Hoppy, in his enthusiasm, had bought no less than one hundred and forty tortoises and he carried them home in baskets, ten or fifteen at a time. He had to make a lot of trips and he was quite exhausted at the end of it all, but it was worth it. Boy, was it worth it! And what an amazing sight his living room was when they were all in there together! The floor was swarming with tortoises of different sizes, some walking slowly about and exploring, some munching cabbage leaves, others drinking water from a big shallow dish. They made just the faintest rustling sound as they moved over the canvas sheet, but that was all. Mr. Hoppy had to pick his way carefully on his toes between this moving sea of brown shells whenever he walked across the room. But enough of that. He must get on with the job."

One hundred and forty tortoises sure is a lot! Use the space below to draw as many tortoises as you can, each a different size, shape, color, and pattern from the others.

Alfie's House

"Alfie's weight was thirteen ounces. Tortoise Number 8 was twenty-seven ounces. Very slowly, over seven weeks, Mrs. Silver's pet had more than doubled in size and the good lady hadn't noticed a thing.

Even to Mr. Hoppy, peering down over his railing, Tortoise Number 8 looked pretty big. It was amazing that Mrs. Silver had hardly noticed anything at all during the great operation. Only once had she looked up and said, "You know, Mr. Hoppy, I do believe he's getting a bit bigger. What do you think?"

"I can't see a lot of difference myself," Mr. Hoppy had answered casually.

But now perhaps it was time to call a halt, and that evening Mr. Hoppy was just about to go out and suggest to Mrs. Silver that she ought to weigh Alfie when a startled cry from the balcony below brought him outside fast.

"Look!" Mrs. Silver was shouting. "Alfie's too big to get through the door of his little house! He must have grown enormously!"

"Weigh him," Mr. Hoppy ordered. "Take him in and weigh him quick. "

Tortoise Number 8 must be huge! He can't even fit in Alfie's house. Draw the too-small house next to Tortoise Number 8 in the space below.

JAMES'S AUNT SPONGE AND AUNT SPIKER

"Poor James . . . was sent away to live with his two aunts.

Their names were Aunt Sponge and Aunt Spiker, and I am sorry to say that they were both really horrible people. They were selfish and lazy and cruel, and right from the beginning they started beating poor James for almost no reason at all. They never called him by his real name, but always referred to him as "you disgusting little beast" or "you filthy nuisance" or "you miserable creature" and they certainly never gave him any toys to play with or any picture books to look at. His room was as bare as a prison cell.

They lived—Aunt Sponge, Aunt Spiker, and now James as well—in a queer ramshackle house on the top of a high hill in the south of England.

✳ ✳ ✳

It all started on a blazing hot day in the middle of summer. Aunt Sponge, Aunt Spiker, and James were all out in the garden. James had been put to work, as usual. This time he was chopping wood for the kitchen stove. Aunt Sponge and Aunt Spiker were sitting comfortably in deck chairs nearby, sipping tall glasses of fizzy lemonade and watching him to see that he didn't stop work for one moment.

Aunt Sponge was enormously fat and very short. She had small piggy eyes, a sunken mouth, and one of those white flabby faces that looked exactly as though it had been boiled. She was like a great white soggy overboiled cabbage. Aunt Spiker, on the other hand, was lean and tall and bony, and she wore steel-rimmed spectacles that fixed onto the end of her nose with a clip. She had a screeching voice and long wet narrow lips, and whenever she got angry or excited, little flecks of spit would come shooting out of her mouth as she talked. And there they sat, these two ghastly hags, sipping their drinks, and every now and again screaming at James to chop faster and faster. They also talked about themselves, each one saying how beautiful she thought she was. Aunt Sponge had a long-handled mirror on her lap, and she kept picking it up and gazing at her own hideous face. "

It's hard to imagine two such horrible people as Aunt Sponge and Aunt Spiker!
Draw them sitting in the space below, while poor James chops the wood
as fast as he possibly can.

James and the Old Man

"It was at this point that the first thing of all, the *rather* peculiar thing that led to so many other *much* more peculiar things, happened to him.

For suddenly, just behind him, James heard a rustling of leaves, and he turned around and saw an old man in a crazy dark-green suit emerging from the bushes. He was a very small old man, but he had a huge bald head and a face that was covered all over with bristly black whiskers. He stopped when he was about three yards away, and he stood there leaning on his stick and staring hard at James."

Indeed, what a rather peculiar thing! Draw the small old man in his crazy dark-green suit standing next to James in the space below.

INSIDE THE GIANT PEACH

"Then he noticed that there was a small door cut into the face of the peach stone. He gave a push. It swung open. He crawled through it, and before he had time to glance up and see where he was, he heard a voice saying, "*Look who's here!*" And another one said,

"We've been waiting for you!"

James stopped and stared at the speakers, his face white with horror.

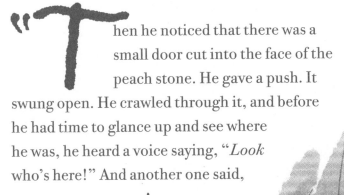

He started to stand up, but his knees were shaking so much he had to sit down again on the floor. He glanced behind him, thinking he could bolt back into the tunnel the way he had come, but the doorway had disappeared. There was now only a solid brown wall behind him.

✳ ✳ ✳

James's large frightened eyes traveled slowly around the room.

The creatures, some sitting on chairs, others reclining on a sofa, were all watching him intently.

Creatures?

Or were they insects?

An insect is usually something rather small, is it not? A grasshopper, for example, is an insect.

So what would you call it if you saw a grasshopper as large as a dog? As large as a *large* dog. You could hardly call *that* an insect, could you?

There was an Old-Green-Grasshopper as large as a large dog sitting on a stool directly across the room from James now.

And next to the Old-Green-Grasshopper, there was an enormous Spider.

And next to the Spider, there was a giant Ladybug with nine black spots on her scarlet shell.

Each of these three was squatting upon a magnificent chair.

On a sofa nearby, reclining comfortably in curled-up positions, there was a Centipede and an Earthworm.

On the floor over in the far corner, there was something thick and white that looked as though it might be a Silkworm. But it was sleeping soundly and nobody was paying any attention to it.

Every one of these "creatures" was at least as big as James himself, and in the strange greenish light that shone down from somewhere in the ceiling, they were absolutely terrifying to behold. "

Draw each of the creatures lounging around in the space below—the Old-Green-Grasshopper in the great big chair, with the Spider,

the Ladybug,

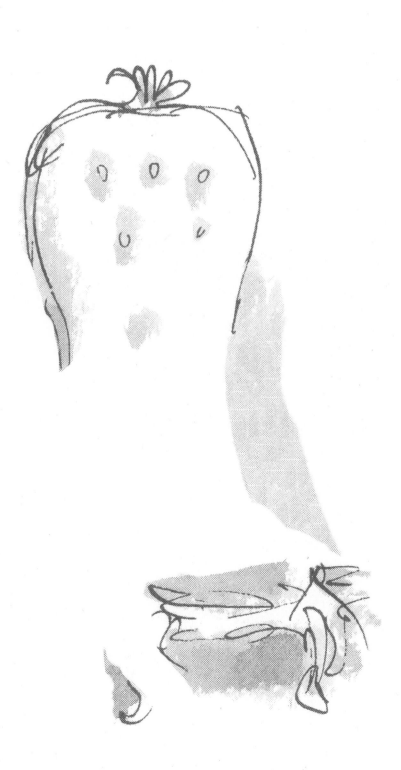

the Centipede,

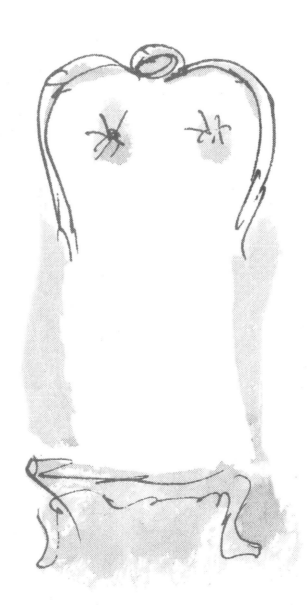

and the Earthworm.

Where is the Silkworm?

The Boots of a Centipede

"And meanwhile, I wish you'd come over here and give me a hand with these boots. It takes me *hours* to get them all off by myself."

✳ ✳ ✳

James decided that this was most certainly not a time to be disagreeable, so he crossed the room to where the Centipede was sitting and knelt down beside him.

"Thank you so much," the Centipede said. "You are very kind."

"You have a lot of boots," James murmured.

"I have a lot of legs," the Centipede answered proudly. "And a lot of feet. One hundred, to be exact."

"*There* he goes again!" the Earthworm cried, speaking for the first time. "He simply cannot stop telling lies about his legs! He doesn't have anything *like* a hundred of them! He's only got forty-two! The trouble is that most people don't bother to count them. They just take his word. And anyway, there is nothing *marvelous*, you know, Centipede, about having a lot of legs."

Does the Centipede *really* have one hundred legs? Draw a boot on each of his legs in the picture below.

SHARK ATTACK ON THE GIANT PEACH

FROM JAMES AND THE GIANT PEACH

"Look!" cried the Centipede just as they were finishing their meal. "Look at that funny thin black thing gliding through the water over there!"

They all swung around to look.

"There are two of them," said Miss Spider.

"There are *lots* of them!" said the Ladybug.

"What are they?" asked the Earthworm, getting worried.

"They must be some kind of fish," said the Old-Green-Grasshopper. "Perhaps they have come along to say hello."

"They are sharks!" cried the Earthworm. "I'll bet you anything you like that they are sharks and they have come along to eat us up!"

"What absolute rot!" the Centipede said, but his voice seemed suddenly to have become a little shaky, and he wasn't laughing.

"I am *positive* they are sharks!" said the Earthworm. "I just *know* they are sharks!"

And so, in actual fact, did everybody else, but they were too frightened to admit it.

There was a short silence. They all peered down anxiously at the sharks, who were cruising slowly round and round the peach.

"Just assuming that they *are* sharks," the Centipede said, "there still can't possibly be any danger if we stay up here."

But even as he spoke, one of those thin black fins suddenly changed direction and came cutting swiftly through the water right up to the side of the peach itself. The shark paused and stared up at the company with small evil eyes.

"Go away!" they shouted. "Go away, you filthy beast!"

Slowly, almost lazily, the shark opened his mouth (which was big enough to have swallowed a perambulator) and made a lunge at the peach.

They all watched, aghast.

And now, as though at a signal from the leader, all the other sharks came swimming in toward the peach, and they clustered around it and began to attack it furiously. There must have been twenty or thirty of them at least, all pushing and fighting and lashing their tails and churning the water into a froth.

Panic and pandemonium broke out immediately on top of the peach.

"Oh, we are finished now!" cried Miss Spider, wringing her feet. "They will eat up the whole peach and then there'll be nothing left for us to stand on and they'll start on us!"

"She is right!" shouted the Ladybug. "We are lost forever!"

What are James and the creatures going to do? Draw the sharks biting at the enormous peach, while James and his friends watch terrified from above.

Painting a Rainbow

"Once, as they drifted silently past a massive white cloud, they saw on the top of it a group of strange, tall, wispy-looking things that were about twice the height of ordinary men. They were not easy to see at first because they were almost as white as the cloud itself, but as the peach sailed closer, it became obvious that these "things" were actually living creatures—tall, wispy, wraithlike, shadowy white creatures who looked as though they were made out of a mixture of cotton-wool and candy-floss and thin white hairs.

"Ooooooooooooooh!" the Ladybug said. "I don't like this at all!"

"Ssshh!" James whispered back. "Don't let them hear you! They must be Cloud-Men!"

They all had huge brushes in their hands and they were splashing the paint onto the great curvy arch in a frenzy of speed, so fast, in fact, that in a few minutes the whole of the arch became covered with the most glorious colors—reds, blues, greens, yellows, and purples.

"It's a rainbow!" everyone said at once. "They are making a rainbow!"

The Cloud-Men do paint the most beautiful rainbows! Draw the colorful rainbow the Cloud-Men are painting in the space below.

MATILDA'S PARENTS

"**H**aving got the address from school records, Miss Honey set out to walk from her own home to the Wormwoods' house shortly after nine. She found the house in a pleasant street where each smallish building was separated from its neighbors by a bit of garden. It was a modern brick house that could not have been cheap to buy and the name on the gate said COSY NOOK. Nosey cook might have been better, Miss Honey thought. She was given to playing with words in that way. She walked up the path and rang the bell, and while she stood waiting she could hear the television blaring inside.

They were in the living room eating their suppers on their knees in front of the telly. The suppers were TV dinners in floppy aluminum containers with separate compartments for the stewed meat, the boiled potatoes, and the peas. Mrs. Wormwood sat munching her meal with her eyes glued to the American soap-opera on the screen. She was a large woman whose hair was dyed platinum blond except where you could see the mousy-brown bits growing out from the roots. She wore heavy makeup and she had one of those unfortunate bulging figures where the flesh appears to be strapped in all around the body to prevent it from falling out.

✳ ✳ ✳

Mr. Wormwood was a small ratty-looking man whose front teeth stuck out underneath a thin ratty moustache. He liked to wear jackets with large brightly-colored checks and he sported ties that were usually yellow or pale green."

Sometimes Matilda wonders just *how* she could be related to her terrible parents. They don't like to read, they don't ask questions, and they spend all their time in front of the telly! Draw Mr. and Mrs. Wormwood sitting on their chairs eating dinner from their knees.

"Mr. Wormwood didn't notice anything when he put the hat on, but when he arrived at the garage he couldn't get it off. Superglue is very powerful stuff, so powerful it will take your skin off if you pull too hard. Mr. Wormwood didn't want to be scalped so he had to keep the hat on his head the whole day long, even when putting sawdust in gear-boxes and fiddling the mileages of cars with his electric drill. In an effort to save face, he adopted a casual attitude hoping that his staff would think that he actually *meant* to keep his hat on all day long just for the heck of it, like gangsters do in the films.

When he got home that evening he still couldn't get the hat off. "Don't be silly," his wife said. "Come here. I'll take it off for you."

Mrs. Wormwood pulled and pulled and pulled, but she couldn't get the hat off!
Draw Mrs. Wormwood trying to get the hat off her husband's head.

MATILDA AND CRUNCHEM HALL

"Matilda longed for her parents to be good and loving and understanding and honorable and intelligent. The fact that they were none of these things was something she had to put up with. It was not easy to do so. But the new game she had invented of punishing one or both of them each time they were beastly to her made her life more or less bearable.

Being very small and very young, the only power Matilda had over anyone in her family was brain-power.

For sheer cleverness she could run rings around them all. But the fact remained that any five-year-old girl in any family was always obliged to do as she was told, however asinine the orders might be. Thus she was always forced to eat her evening meals out of TV-dinner-trays in front of the dreaded box. She always had to stay alone on weekday afternoons, and whenever she was told to shut up, she had to shut up.

✳ ✳ ✳

Matilda was a little late in starting school. Most children begin Primary School at five or even just before, but Matilda's parents, who weren't very concerned one way or the other about their daughter's education, had forgotten to make the proper arrangements in advance. She was five and a half when she entered school for the first time.

The village school for younger children was a bleak brick building called Crunchem Hall Primary School. It had about two hundred and fifty pupils aged from five to just under twelve years old. The head teacher, the boss, the supreme commander of this establishment was a formidable middle-aged lady whose name was Miss Trunchbull.

Naturally Matilda was put in the bottom class, where there were eighteen other small boys and girls about the same age as her. Their teacher was called Miss Honey . . . "

Now that Matilda is *finally* allowed to go to school, she can learn all she wants! What do her classmates look like? Draw in some of Matilda's new friends sitting at their desks.

Miss Honey

"She could not have been more than twenty-three or twenty-four. She had a lovely pale oval madonna face with blue eyes and her hair was light-brown. Her body was so slim and fragile one got the feeling that if she fell over she would smash into a thousand pieces, like a porcelain figure.

Miss Jennifer Honey was a mild and quiet person who never raised her voice and was seldom seen to smile, but there is no doubt she possessed that rare gift for being adored by every small child under her care. She seemed to understand totally the bewilderment and fear that so often overwhelms young children who for the first time in their lives are herded into a classroom and told to obey orders. Some curious warmth that was almost tangible shone out of Miss Honey's face when she spoke to a confused and homesick newcomer to the class."

How lovely to have a teacher such as Miss Honey! She must be the best teacher in the world. Draw Miss Honey in the space below.

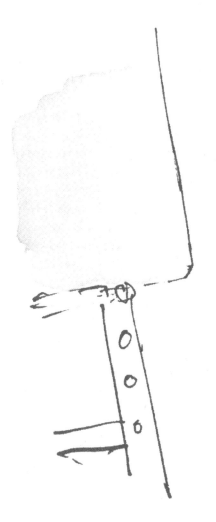

THE CHOCOLATE CAKE

"When she spoke again her voice was suddenly softer, quieter, more friendly, and she leaned towards the boy, smiling. "You like my special chocolate cake, don't you, Bogtrotter? It's rich and delicious, isn't it, Bogtrotter?"

"Very good," the boy mumbled. The words were out before he could stop himself.

"You're right," the Trunchbull said. "It *is* very good. Therefore I think you should congratulate the cook. When a gentleman has had a particularly good meal, Bogtrotter, he always sends his compliments to the chef. You didn't know that, did you, Bogtrotter? But those who inhabit the criminal underworld are not noted for their good manners."

The boy remained silent.

"Cook!" the Trunchbull shouted, turning her head towards the door.

"Come here, cook! Bogtrotter wishes to tell you how good your chocolate cake is!"

✳ ✳ ✳

The cake was fully eighteen inches in diameter and it was covered with dark-brown chocolate icing. "Put it on the table," the Trunchbull said.

There was a small table center stage with a chair behind it. The cook placed the cake carefully on the table. "Sit down, Bogtrotter," the Trunchbull said. "Sit there."

The boy moved cautiously to the table and sat down. He stared at the gigantic cake.

✳ ✳ ✳

Very gingerly the boy began to cut a thin slice of the vast cake. Then he levered the slice out. Then he put down the knife and took the sticky thing in his fingers and started very slowly to eat it.

"It's good, isn't it?" the Trunchbull asked.

"Very good," the boy said, chewing and swallowing. He finished the slice.

"Have another," the Trunchbull said.

"That's enough, thank you," the boy murmured.

"I said have another," the Trunchbull said, and now there was an altogether sharper edge to her voice. "Eat another slice! Do as you are told!"

"I don't want another slice," the boy said.

Suddenly the Trunchbull exploded. "Eat!" she shouted, banging her thigh with the riding-crop. "If I tell you to eat, you will eat! You wanted cake!

You stole cake! And now you've got cake! What's more, you're going to eat it! You do not leave this platform and nobody leaves this hall until you have eaten the entire cake that is sitting there in front of you! Do I make myself clear, Bogtrotter? Do you get my meaning?"

The boy looked at the Trunchbull. Then he looked down at the enormous cake.

"Eat! Eat! Eat!" the Trunchbull was yelling.

Very slowly the boy cut himself another slice and began to eat it."

The cook has made one great big cake for a boy to eat all by himself—is he ever going to finish it? Draw Bruce Bogtrotter trying to eat the huge chocolate cake in the space below, while the Trunchbull watches over him.

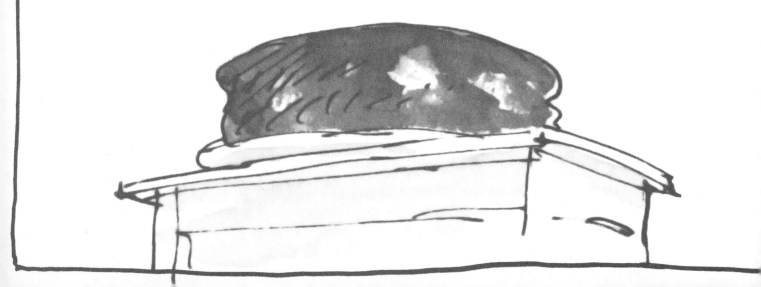

Matilda and the Parrot

"Fred was a friend of Matilda's. He was a small boy of six who lived just around the corner from her, and for days he had been going on about this great talking parrot his father had given him.

So the following afternoon, as soon as Mrs. Wormwood had departed in her car for another session of bingo, Matilda set out for Fred's house to investigate. She knocked on his door and asked if he would be kind enough to show her the famous bird. Fred was delighted and led her up to his bedroom where a truly magnificent blue and yellow parrot sat in a tall cage."

Rattle my bones, it's a talking parrot! Draw the beautiful bird sitting on its perch in the cage.

THROWING THE HAMMER

"**M**iss Trunchbull, the Headmistress, was something else altogether. She was a gigantic holy terror, a fierce tyrannical monster who frightened the life out of the pupils and teachers alike.

✳ ✳ ✳

Matilda and Lavender saw the giant in green breeches advancing upon a girl of about ten who had a pair of plaited golden pigtails hanging over her shoulders. Each pigtail had a blue satin bow at the end of it and it all looked very pretty. The girl wearing the pigtails, Amanda Thripp, stood quite still, watching the advancing giant, and the expression on her face was one that you might find on the face of a person who is trapped in a small field with an enraged bull which is charging flat-out towards her. The girl was glued to the spot, terror-struck, pop-eyed, quivering, knowing for certain that the Day of Judgment had come for her at last.

Miss Trunchbull had now reached the victim and stood towering over her.

"I want those filthy pigtails off before you come back to school tomorrow!" she barked.

"Chop 'em off and throw 'em in the dustbin, you understand?"

Amanda, paralyzed with fright, managed to stutter, "My m-m-mummy likes them. She p-p-plaits them for me every morning."

"Your mummy's a twit!" the Trunchbull bellowed. She pointed a finger the size of a salami at the child's head and shouted, "You look like a rat with a tail coming out of its head!"

"My m-m-mummy thinks I look lovely, Miss T-T-Trunchbull," Amanda stuttered, shaking like a blancmange.

"I don't give a tinker's toot what your mummy thinks!" the Trunchbull yelled, and with that she lunged forward and grabbed hold of Amanda's pigtails in her right fist and lifted the girl clear off the ground. Then she started swinging her round and round her head, faster and faster and Amanda was screaming blue murder and the Trunchbull was yelling, "I'll give you pigtails, you little rat!"

"Shades of the Olympics," Hortensia murmured. "She's getting up speed now, just like she does with the hammer. Ten to one she's going to throw her."

And now the Trunchbull was leaning back against the weight of the whirling girl and pivoting expertly on her toes, spinning round and round, and soon Amanda Thripp was traveling so fast she became a blur, and suddenly, with a mighty grunt, the Trunchbull let go of the pigtails and Amanda went sailing like a rocket right over the wire fence of the playground and high up into the sky. **"**

The Trunchbull has done it this time—she's sent a student soaring! Draw Amanda Thripp with her pigtails trailing as she sails through the sky.

The Terrifying Trunchbull

"The Trunchbull, this mighty female giant, stood there in her green breeches, quivering like a blancmange. She was especially furious that someone had succeeded in making her jump and yell like that because she prided herself on her toughness.

✳ ✳ ✳

She looked at this moment more terrifying than ever before. The fires of fury and hatred were smoldering in her small black eyes. "

The Trunchbull is as mad as she's ever been! Draw the frightening woman towering over her students.

MR. AND MRS. TWIT

"Mr. Twit was one of these very hairy-faced men. The whole of his face except for his forehead, his eyes, and his nose, was covered with thick hair. The stuff even sprouted in revolting tufts out of his nostrils and ear-holes.

Mr. Twit felt that this hairiness made him look terrifically wise and grand. But in truth he was neither of these things.

Mr. Twit was a twit. He was born a twit. And now at the age of sixty, he was a bigger twit than ever.

The hair on Mr. Twit's face didn't grow smooth and matted as it does on most hairy-faced men. It grew in spikes that stuck out straight like the bristles of a nailbrush.

And how often did Mr. Twit wash this bristly nailbrushy face of his?

The answer is NEVER, not even on Sundays.

He hadn't washed it for years.

✳ ✳ ✳

Mr. Twit didn't even bother to open his mouth wide when he ate. As a result (and because he never washed) there were always hundreds of bits of old breakfasts and lunches and suppers sticking to the hairs around his face. They weren't big bits, mind you, because he used to wipe those off with the back of his hand or on his sleeve while he was eating. But if you looked closely (not that you'd ever want to) you would see tiny little specks of dried-up scrambled eggs stuck to the hairs, and spinach and tomato ketchup and fishsticks and minced chicken livers and all the other disgusting things Mr. Twit liked to eat.

✳ ✳ ✳

Mrs. Twit was no better than her husband.

She did not, of course, have a hairy face. It was a pity she didn't because that, at any rate, would have hidden some of her fearful ugliness.

Take a look at her.

Have you ever seen a woman with an uglier face than that? I doubt it.

But the funny thing is that Mrs. Twit wasn't born ugly. She'd had quite a nice face when she was young. The ugliness had grown upon her year by year as she got older.

Why would that happen? I'll tell you why.

If a person has ugly thoughts, it begins to show on the face. And when that person has ugly thoughts every day, every week, every year, the face gets uglier and uglier until it gets so ugly you can hardly bear to look at it.

A person who has good thoughts cannot ever be ugly. You can have a wonky nose and a crooked mouth and a double chin and stick-out teeth, but if you have good thoughts they will shine out of your face like sunbeams and you will always look lovely.

Nothing good shone out of Mrs. Twit's face.

In her right hand she carried a walking stick. She used to tell people that this was because she had warts growing on the sole of her left foot and walking was painful. But the real reason she carried a stick was so that she could hit things with it, things like dogs and cats and small children.

And then there was the glass eye. Mrs. Twit had a glass eye that was always looking the other way."

The Twits are mean and miserable people, and it shows on their mean and miserable faces. Draw Mr. Twit's big, hairy face in the space below.

What nasty things does Mr. Twit have stuck in his beard? Food? Plants? Bugs? Draw bits stuck in his big dirty beard below.

Draw Mrs. Twit's unhairy (but very ugly) face in the space below.

And what about the glass eye? Mrs. Twit's terrifying glass eye!
Draw it in the space below.

"**H**ere is a picture of Mr. and Mrs. Twit's house and garden. Some house! It looks like a prison. And not a window anywhere.

"Who wants windows?" Mr. Twit had said when they were building it. "Who wants every Tom, Dick, and Harry peeping in to see what you're doing?" It didn't occur to Mr. Twit that windows were meant mainly for looking out of, not for looking into.

And what do you think of that ghastly garden? Mrs. Twit was the gardener. She was very good at growing thistles and stinging-nettles. "I always grow plenty of spiky thistles and plenty of stinging-nettles," she used to say. "They keep out nasty, nosy little children."

Near the house you can see Mr. Twit's workshed.

To one side there is The Big Dead Tree. It never has any leaves on it because it's dead. "

What a sad house the Twits have. No windows, and only a dead tree? Draw the ugly little house, the workshed, and Mrs. Twit's spiky garden around it.

FOUR STICKY LITTLE BOYS

"On one Tuesday evening after Mr. Twit had been up the ladder and smeared the tree with HUGTIGHT, four little boys crept into the garden to look at the monkeys. They didn't care about the thistles and stinging-nettles, not when there were monkeys to look at. After a while, they got tired of looking at the monkeys, so they explored further into the garden and found the ladder leaning against The Big Dead Tree. They decided to climb it just for fun.

There's nothing wrong with that.

The next morning, when Mr. Twit went out to collect the birds, he found four miserable little boys sitting in the tree, stuck as tight as could be by the seats of their pants to the branches. There were no birds because the presence of the boys had scared them away.

Mr. Twit was furious. "As there are no birds for my pie tonight," he shouted, "then it'll have to be *boys* instead!" He started to climb the ladder. "Boy Pie might be better than Bird Pie," he went on, grinning horribly. "More meat and not so many tiny little bones!"

The boys were terrified. "He's going to boil us!" cried one of them.

"He'll stew us alive!" wailed the second one.

"He'll cook us with carrots!" cried the third.

But the fourth little boy, who had more sense than the others, whispered,

"Listen, I've just had an idea. We are only stuck by the seats of our pants. So quick! Unbutton your pants and slip out of them and fall to the ground."

Mr. Twit had reached the top of the ladder and was just about to make a grab for the nearest boy when they all suddenly tumbled out of the tree and ran for home with their naked bottoms winking at the sun."

Those boys were lucky to escape with their bottoms still attached! They very nearly could have been inside a pie. Draw the four boys glued by the seats of their pants to **The Big Dead Tree**.

Mrs. Twit Goes Ballooning

"**M**r. Twit led Mrs. Twit outdoors where he had everything ready for the great stretching.

He had one hundred balloons and lots of string.

He had a gas cylinder for filling the balloons.

He had fixed an iron ring into the ground.

"Stand here," he said, pointing to the iron ring. He then tied Mrs. Twit's ankles to the iron ring.

When that was done, he began filling the balloons with gas. Each balloon was on a long string and when it was filled with gas it pulled on its string, trying to go up and up. Mr. Twit tied the ends of the strings to the top half of Mrs. Twit's body. Some he tied around her neck, some under her arms, some to her wrists, and some even to her hair.

Soon there were fifty colored balloons floating in the air above Mrs. Twit's head.

"Put some more string around my ankles quickly! I want to feel absolutely safe!"

"Very well, my angel," said Mr. Twit, and with a ghoulish grin on his lips he knelt down at her feet. He took a knife from his pocket and with one quick slash he cut through the strings holding Mrs. Twit's ankles to the iron ring.

She went up like a rocket.

"Help!" she screamed. "Save me!"

But there was no saving her now. In a few seconds she was high up in the blue blue sky and climbing fast. **"**

Show Mrs. Twit flying skyward with fifty balloons attached to her.

Bird Pie

"Once a week, on Wednesdays, the Twits had Bird Pie for supper. Mr. Twit caught the birds and Mrs. Twit cooked them.

Mr. Twit was good at catching birds. On the day before Bird Pie day, he would put the ladder up against The Big Dead Tree and climb into the branches with a bucket of glue and a paintbrush.

The glue he used was something called HUGTIGHT and it was stickier than any other glue in the world. He would paint it along the tops of all the branches and then go away.

As the sun went down, birds would fly in from all around to roost for the night in The Big Dead Tree. They didn't know, poor things, that the branches were all smeared with horrible HUGTIGHT. The moment they landed on a branch, their feet stuck and that was that.

The next morning, which was Bird Pie day, Mr. Twit would climb up the ladder again and grab all the wretched birds that were stuck to the tree. It didn't matter what kind they were–song thrushes, blackbirds, sparrows, crows, little jenny wrens, robins, anything–they all went into the pot for Wednesday's Bird Pie supper.

Mrs. Twit's Bird Pie sounds truly disgusting. Does she even remove their feet and their beaks before she cooks them? Draw the steaming Bird Pie in the space below.

The Great Upside-Down Monkey Circus

"Now for the monkeys.

The four monkeys in the cage in the garden were all one family. They were Muggle-Wump and his wife and their two small children.

But what on earth were Mr. and Mrs. Twit doing with monkeys in their garden?

Well, in the old days, they had both worked in a circus as monkey trainers. They used to teach monkeys to do tricks and to dress up in human clothes and to smoke pipes and all the rest of that nonsense.

Today, although they were retired, Mr. Twit still wanted to train monkeys. It was his dream that one day he would own the first GREAT UPSIDE-DOWN MONKEY CIRCUS in the world.

That meant that the monkeys had to do everything upside down. They had to dance upside down (on their hands with their feet in the air). They had to play football upside down. They had to balance one on top of the other upside down, with Muggle-Wump at the bottom and the smallest baby monkey at the very top. They even had to eat and drink upside down and that is not an easy thing to do because the food and water has to go *up* your throat instead of down it. In fact, it is almost impossible, but the monkeys simply had to do it otherwise they got nothing.

All this sounds pretty silly to you and me. It sounded pretty silly to the monkeys, too. They absolutely hated having to do this upside-down nonsense day after day. It made them giddy standing on their heads for hours on end. Sometimes the two small monkey children would faint with so much blood going to their heads. But Mr. Twit didn't care about that. He kept them practicing for six hours every day and if they didn't do as they were told, Mrs. Twit would soon come running with her beastly stick. "

The poor monkeys are fed up with all of this training! They don't *want* to be in a circus. Draw them practicing their upside-down act in the space below.

The Roly-Poly Bird

"**T**hen one day, a truly magnificent bird flew down out of the sky and landed on the monkey cage.

"Good heavens!" cried all the monkeys together. "It's the Roly-Poly Bird! What on earth are you doing over here in England, Roly-Poly Bird?" Like the monkeys, the Roly-Poly Bird came from Africa, and he spoke the same language as they did. "

Thank goodness for the Roly-Poly Bird! Draw the beautiful bird, with his great big feathers and lovely wings, sitting on top of the monkey cage.

SPACE HOTEL "U.S.A"

"Mr. Wonka's Great Glass Elevator was not the only thing orbiting the earth at that particular time. Two days earlier, the United States of America had successfully launched its first Space Hotel, a gigantic sausage-shaped capsule no less than one thousand feet long. It was called Space Hotel "U.S.A." and it was the marvel of the space age. It had inside it a tennis court, a swimming pool, a gymnasium, a children's playroom, and five hundred luxury bedrooms, each with a private bath. It was fully air-conditioned. It was also equipped with a gravity-making machine so that you didn't float about inside it. You could walk normally.

This extraordinary object was now speeding round and round the earth at a height of two hundred and forty miles. Guests were to be taken up and down by a taxi service of commuter capsules blasting off from Cape Kennedy every hour on the hour, Monday through Friday. But as yet there was nobody on board at all, not even an astronaut. The reason for this was that no one had really believed such an enormous thing would ever get off the ground without blowing up.

But the launching had been a great success and now that the Space Hotel was safely in orbit, there was a tremendous hustle and bustle to send up the first guests. It was rumored that the President of the United States himself was going to be among the first to stay in the hotel, and of course there was a mad rush by all sorts of other people across the world to book rooms. Several kings and queens had cabled the White House in Washington for reservations, and a Texas millionaire called Orson Cart, who was about to marry a Hollywood starlet called Helen Highwater, was offering one hundred thousand dollars a day for the honeymoon suite.

But you cannot send guests to a hotel unless there are lots of people there to look after them, and that explains why there was yet another interesting object orbiting the earth at that moment. This was the large Commuter Capsule containing the entire staff for Space Hotel "U.S.A." There were managers, assistant managers, desk clerks, waitresses, bellhops, chambermaids, pastry chefs, and hall porters. The capsule they were traveling in was manned by the three famous astronauts, Shuckworth, Shanks, and Showler, all of them handsome, clever, and brave.

"In exactly one hour," said Shuckworth, speaking to the passengers over the loudspeaker, "we shall link up with Space Hotel 'U.S.A.,' your happy home for the next ten years. And any moment now, if you look straight ahead, you should catch your first glimpse of this magnificent spaceship.

Ah-ha! I see something there! That must be it, folks! There's definitely something up there ahead of us!"

Draw the inside of the great Space Hotel "U.S.A." You could draw a tennis court, a swimming pool, a gymnasium, a children's playroom, or one of the five hundred luxury bedrooms, each with a private bath! What else do you think there would be in a hotel in space?

The Vermicious Knids

"In the lobby of the Space Hotel, Mr. Wonka had merely paused in order to think up another verse, and he was just about to start off again when a frightful piercing scream stopped him cold. The screamer was Grandma Josephine. She was sitting up in bed and pointing with a shaking finger at the elevators at the far end of the lobby. She screamed a second time, still pointing, and all eyes turned toward the elevators. The door of the one on the left was sliding slowly open and the watchers could clearly see that there was something . . . something thick . . . something brown . . . something not exactly brown, but greenish-brown . . . something with slimy skin and large eyes . . . squatting inside the elevator!

✳ ✳ ✳

It looked more than anything like an enormous egg balanced on its pointed end. It was as tall as a big boy and wider than the fattest man. The greenish-brown skin had a shiny wettish appearance and there were wrinkles in it. About three-quarters up, in the widest part, there were two large round eyes as big as teacups. The eyes were white, but each had a brilliant red pupil in the center. The red pupils were resting on Mr. Wonka. **"**

It's a Vermicious Knid! It looks ready to flocculate your bones and rasp you alive! Draw the Vermicious Knid in the elevator.

INSIDE THE GREAT GLASS ELEVATOR

"Bunkum and tummyrot! You'll never get anywhere if you go about what-iffing like that. Would Columbus have discovered America if he'd said 'What if I sink on the way over? What if I meet pirates? What if I never come back?' He wouldn't even have started! We want no what-iffers around here, right Charlie? Off we go, then! But wait . . . this is a very tricky maneuver and I'm going to need help. We have to press lots of buttons, all in different parts of the Elevator. I shall take those two over there, the white and the black." Mr. Wonka made a funny blowing noise with his mouth and glided effortlessly, like a huge bird, across the Elevator to the white and black buttons, and there he hovered. "Grandpa Joe, sir, kindly station yourself beside that silver button there . . . yes, that's the one. And you, Charlie, go up and stay floating beside that little golden button near the ceiling. I must tell you that each of these buttons fires booster rockets from different places outside the Elevator. That's how we change direction. Grandpa Joe's rockets turn us to starboard, to the right. Charlie's turn us to port, to the left. Mine make us go higher or lower or faster or slower. All ready?"

"No! Wait!" cried Charlie, who was floating exactly midway between the floor and the ceiling. "How do I get up? I can't get up to the ceiling!" He was thrashing his arms and legs violently, like a drowning swimmer, but getting nowhere.

"My dear boy," said Mr. Wonka. "You can't *swim* in this stuff. It isn't water you know. It's air, and very thin air at that. There's nothing to push against. So you have to use jet propulsion. Watch me. First, you take a deep breath, then you make a small round hole with your mouth and you blow as hard as you can. If you blow downward, you jet propel yourself up. If you blow left, you shoot off to the right, and so on. You maneuver yourself like a spacecraft, but using your mouth as a booster rocket."

Suddenly everyone began practicing this business of flying about, and the whole Elevator was filled with the blowings and snortings of the passengers. Grandma Georgina, in her red flannel nightgown with two skinny bare legs sticking out of the bottom was trumpeting and spitting like a rhinoceros and flying from one side of the Elevator to the other, shouting, "Out of my way! Out of my way!" and crashing into poor Mr. and Mrs. Bucket with terrible speed. Grandpa George and Grandma Josephine were doing the same."

There is chaos inside the Great Glass Elevator! Draw Charlie, Grandpa Joe, and Grandma Georgina as they rocket around the elevator using their mouths as booster rockets.

"Charlie glanced quickly back at the Commuter Capsule. The sheet-white faces of Shuckworth, Shanks, and Showler were pressed against the glass of the little windows, terror-struck, stupefied, stunned, their mouths open, their expressions frozen like fishfingers. Once again, Charlie gave them the thumbs-up signal. Showler acknowledged it with a sickly grin, but that was all."

Shuckworth, Shanks, and Showler are cowering at the sight of the Knids. Draw the three astronauts in their space capsule.

THE MAGIC FINGER AND MRS. WINTER

"**T**he Magic Finger is something I have been able to do all my life.

I can't tell you just *how* I do it, because I don't even know myself.

But it always happens when I get cross, when I see red . . .

Then I get very, very hot all over . . .

Then the tip of the forefinger of my right hand begins to tingle most terribly . . .

And suddenly a sort of flash comes out of me, a quick flash, like something electric.

It jumps out and touches the person who has made me cross . . .

And after that the Magic Finger is upon him or her, and things begin to happen . . .

For months I had been telling myself that I would never put the Magic Finger upon anyone again–not after what happened to my teacher, old Mrs. Winter.

Poor old Mrs. Winter.

One day we were in class, and she was teaching us spelling. "Stand up," she said to me, "and spell cat."

"That's an easy one," I said. "*K-a-t.*"

"You are a stupid little girl!" Mrs. Winter said.

"I am not a stupid little girl!" I cried. "I am a very nice little girl!"

"Go and stand in the corner," Mrs. Winter said.

Then I got cross, and I saw red, and I put the Magic Finger on Mrs. Winter good and strong, and almost at once . . .

Guess what?

Whiskers began growing out of her face! They were long black whiskers, just like the ones you see on a cat, only much bigger. And how fast they grew! Before we had time to think, they were out to her ears!

Of course the whole class started screaming with laughter, and then Mrs. Winter said, "Will you be so kind as to tell me what you find so madly funny, all of you?"

And when she turned around to write something on the blackboard we saw that she had grown a *tail* as well! It was a huge bushy tail!

I cannot begin to tell you what happened after that, but if any of you are wondering whether Mrs. Winter is quite all right again now, the answer is No. And she never will be. "

Oh dear. What *has* the Magic Finger done to Mrs. Winter? Draw the great big ZAP! coming out of the Magic Finger, and the long whiskers and great big bushy tail coming out of Mrs. Winter.

Mr. Gregg Gets Wings

"When morning came, Mr. Gregg was the first to wake up.

He opened his eyes.

He was about to put out a hand for his watch, to see the time.

But his hand wouldn't come out.

"That's funny," he said. "Where is my hand?"

He lay still, wondering what was up.

Maybe he had hurt that hand in some way?

He tried the other hand.

That wouldn't come out either.

He sat up.

Then, for the first time, he saw what he looked like!

He gave a yell and jumped out of bed.

Mrs. Gregg woke up. And when she saw Mr. Gregg standing there on the floor, *she* gave a yell, too.

For he was now a tiny little man!

He was maybe as tall as the seat of a chair, but no taller.

And where his arms had been, he had a pair of duck's wings instead!"

What is Mr. Gregg going to do with wings for arms? Draw the big, feathered duck's wings sticking out of Mr. Gregg's nightshirt.

THE DUCK HOUSE

"They all looked down, and there below them, in their own garden, they saw four *enormous* wild ducks! The ducks were as big as men, and what is more, they had great long arms, like men, instead of wings.

The ducks were walking in a line to the door of the Greggs' house, swinging their arms and holding their beaks high in the air.

"Stop!" called the tiny Mr. Gregg, flying down low over their heads. "Go away! That's my house!"

The ducks looked up and quacked. The first one put out a hand and opened the door of the house and went in. The others went in after him. The door shut.

* * *

But when they got to the house, they found all the windows and doors closed. There was no way in.

"Just look at that beastly duck cooking at my stove!" cried Mrs. Gregg as she flew past the kitchen window. "How dare she!"

"And look at *that* one holding my lovely gun!" shouted Mr. Gregg.

"One of them is lying in my bed!" yelled William, looking into a top window.

"And one of them is playing with my electric train!" cried Philip.

"Oh, dear! Oh, dear!" said Mrs. Gregg. "They have taken over our whole house! We shall never get it back. And what *are* we going to eat?"

* * *

It must have been at about this time that I, back in my own house, picked up the telephone and tried to call Philip. I wanted to see if the family was all right.

"Hello," I said.

"Quack!" said a voice at the other end.

"Who is it?" I asked.

"Quack-quack!"

"Philip," I said, "is that you?"

"Quack-quack-quack-quack-quack!"

"Oh, stop it!" I said.

Then there came a very funny noise. It was like a bird laughing.

I put down the telephone quickly.

"Oh, that Magic Finger!" I cried. "What *has* it done to my friends?"

Quack!
Quack-quack-quack!
Quack-quack!

These ducks with human arms have made themselves right at home! Draw the ducks taking over the inside of the Greggs' house.

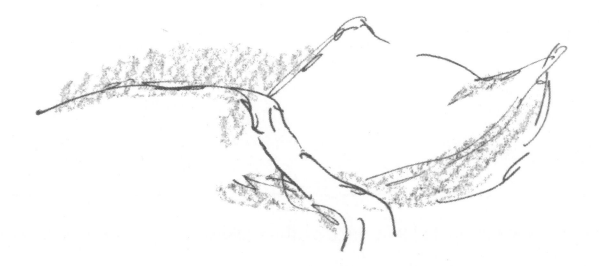

The Greggs Build a Nest

"**M**r. Gregg looked at them and smiled. "We are going to build a nest."

"A nest!" they said. "Can we do that?"

"We *must* do it," said Mr. Gregg. "We've got to have somewhere to sleep. Follow me."

The building of the nest went on and on. It took a long time. But at last it was finished.

"Try it," said Mr. Gregg, hopping back. He was very pleased with his work.

"Oh, isn't it lovely!" cried Mrs. Gregg, going into it and sitting down. "I feel I might lay an egg any moment!"

The others all got in beside her. **"**

The Greggs made the most of it by building themselves a lovely nest. Draw the nest sitting up in this tree in the Greggs' backyard.

DANNY'S OLD GYPSY CARAVAN

"We lived in an old gypsy caravan behind a filling station. My father owned the filling station and the caravan and a small meadow behind, but that was about all he owned in the world. It was a very small filling station on a small country road surrounded by fields and woody hills.

The caravan was our house and our home. It was a real old gypsy wagon with big wheels and fine patterns painted all over it in yellow and red and blue. My father said it was at least one hundred and fifty years old. Many gypsy children, he said, had been born in it and had grown up within its wooden walls. With a horse to pull it, the old caravan must have wandered for thousands of miles along the roads and lanes of England. But now its wanderings were over, and because the wooden spokes in the wheels were beginning to rot, my father had propped it up underneath with bricks.

There was only one room in the caravan, and it wasn't much bigger than a fair-sized modern bathroom. It was a narrow room, the shape of the caravan itself, and against the back wall were two bunk beds, one above the other. The top one was my father's, the bottom one mine.

Although we had electric lights in the workshop, we were not allowed to have them in the caravan. The electricity people said it was unsafe to put wires into something as old and rickety as that. So we got our heat and light in much the same way as the gypsies had done years ago. There was a wood-burning stove with a chimney that went up through the roof, and this kept us warm in winter. There was a kerosene burner on which to boil a kettle or cook a stew, and there was a kerosene lamp hanging from the ceiling.

Immediately behind the caravan was an old apple tree. It bore fine apples that ripened in the middle of September. You could go on picking them for the next four or five weeks. Some of the boughs of the tree hung right over the caravan and when the wind blew the apples down in the night, they often landed on our roof. I would hear them going *thump . . . thump . . . thump . . .* above my head as I lay in my bunk, but those noises never frightened me because I knew exactly what was making them.

I really loved living in that gypsy caravan."

It's a quiet, simple life, but Danny and his father are happy with it. Draw the old wooden gypsy caravan sitting under the apple tree in the space below.

"Mr. Victor Hazell was a roaring snob and he tried desperately to get in with what he believed were the right kind of folk. He hunted with the hounds and gave shooting parties and wore fancy waistcoats. And every weekday he drove his enormous silver Rolls-Royce past our filling station on his way to the brewery. As he flashed by we would sometimes catch a glimpse of the great, glistening beery face above the wheel, pink as a ham, all soft and inflamed from drinking too much beer."

Mr. Hazell is about as stuck-up as they come. Draw Mr. Hazell and his Rolls-Royce as he pulls into Danny's father's filling station.

DANNY LEARNS POACHING

"My father was very tense. He was picking his feet up high and putting them down gently on the brown leaves. He kept his head moving all the time, the eyes sweeping slowly from side to side, searching for danger. I tried doing the same, but soon I began to see a keeper behind every tree, so I gave it up.

We went on like this for maybe four or five minutes, going slowly deeper and deeper into the wood.

Then a large patch of sky appeared ahead of us in the roof of the forest, and I knew that this must be the clearing. My father had told me that the clearing was the place where the young birds were introduced into the wood in early July, where they were fed and watered and guarded by the keepers, and where many of them stayed from force of habit until the shooting began. "There's always plenty of pheasants in the clearing," my father had said.

"And keepers, dad?"

"Yes," he had said. "But there's thick bushes all around and that helps."

The clearing was about one hundred yards ahead of us. We stopped behind a big tree while my father let his eyes rove very slowly all around. He was checking each little shadow and every part of the wood within sight.

"We're going to have to crawl the next bit," he whispered, letting go of my hand. "Keep close behind me all the time, Danny, and do exactly as I do. If you see me lie flat on my face, you do the same. Right?"

"Right," I whispered back.

"Off we go, then. This is it!"

My father got down on his hands and knees and started crawling. I followed. He moved surprisingly fast on all fours and I had quite a job to keep up with him. Every few seconds he would glance back at me to see if I was all right, and each time he did so, I gave him a nod and a smile.

We crawled on and on, and then at last we were kneeling safely behind a big clump of bushes right on the edge of the clearing. My father was nudging me with his elbow and pointing through the branches at the pheasants.

The place was absolutely alive with them. There must have been at least two hundred huge birds strutting around among the tree stumps.

"You see what I mean?" he whispered.

It was a fantastic sight, a sort of poacher's dream come true. And how close they were! Some of them were not ten paces from where we knelt. The hens were plump and creamy-brown. They were so fat their breast feathers almost brushed the ground as they walked. The cocks were slim and elegant, with long tails and brilliant red patches around the eyes, like scarlet spectacles. I glanced at my father. His face was transfixed in ecstasy. The mouth was slightly open and the eyes were sparkling bright as they stared at the pheasants."

Poaching is a very serious and stressful business! Even a pro like Danny's dad needs to be extra careful, especially when Mr. Hazell's land is guarded by keepers. Draw the ground full of pheasants pecking around for food.

Danny Builds a Kite

"There's a good wind today," he said one Saturday morning. "Just right for flying a kite. Let's make a kite, Danny."

So we made a kite. He showed me how to splice four thin sticks together in the shape of a star, with two more sticks across the middle to brace it. Then we cut up an old blue shirt of his and stretched the material across the framework of the kite. We added a long tail made of thread, with little leftover pieces of the shirt tied at intervals along it. We found a ball of string in the workshop, and he showed me how to attach the string to the framework so that the kite would be properly balanced in flight.

Together we walked to the top of the hill behind the filling station to release the kite. I found it hard to believe that this object, made from only a few sticks and a piece of old shirt, would actually fly. I held the string while my father held the kite, and the moment he let it go, it caught the wind and soared upward like a huge blue bird."

Danny and his father have built an excellent kite—it flew straight up into the sky. Draw the blue kite, with its long tail trailing behind it, flying up in the air.

BOGGIS, BUNCE, AND BEAN

"Down in the valley there were three farms. The owners of these farms had done well. They were rich men. They were also nasty men. All three of them were about as nasty and mean as any men you could meet. Their names were Farmer Boggis, Farmer Bunce, and Farmer Bean.

Boggis was a chicken farmer. He kept thousands of chickens. He was enormously fat. This was because he ate three boiled chickens smothered with dumplings every day for breakfast, lunch, and supper.

Bunce was a duck-and-goose farmer. He kept thousands of ducks and geese. He was a kind of pot-bellied dwarf. He was so short his chin would have been underwater in the shallow end of any swimming-pool in the world. His food was doughnuts and goose-livers. He mashed the livers into a disgusting paste and then stuffed the paste into the doughnuts. This diet gave him a tummy-ache and a beastly temper.

Bean was a turkey-and-apple farmer. He kept thousands of turkeys in an orchard full of apple trees. He never ate any food at all. Instead, he drank gallons of strong cider which he made from the apples in his orchard. He was as thin as a pencil and the cleverest of them all.

Boggis and Bunce and Bean
One fat, one short, one lean.
These horrible crooks
So different in looks
Were none the less
equally mean. "

Nasty rich men are Farmers Boggis, Bunce, and Bean. Draw each of them below—fat Boggis eating his chicken, short Bunce standing on a chair to eat his doughnuts, and lean Bean guzzling a jar of cider.

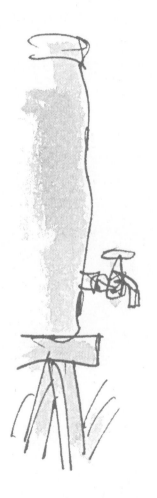

"On a hill above the valley there was a wood.
In the wood there was a huge tree.
Under the tree there was a hole.
In the hole lived Mr. Fox and Mrs. Fox and their four Small Foxes. **"**

Mr. and Mrs. Fox have chosen the best hole under the best tree in all of the farmland to live in. Draw Mr. Fox, Mrs. Fox, and their four Small Foxes standing outside their home.

THE FOXES START DIGGING

"There was no food for the foxes that night, and soon the children dozed off. Then Mrs. Fox dozed off. But Mr. Fox couldn't sleep because of the pain in the stump of his tail. "Well," he thought, "I suppose I'm lucky to be alive at all. And now they've found our hole, we're going to have to move out as soon as possible. We'll never get any peace if we . . . What was *that*?" He turned his head sharply and listened. The noise he heard now was the most frightening noise a fox can ever hear—the scrape-scrape-scraping of shovels digging into the soil.

"Wake up!" he shouted. "They're digging us out!"

Mrs. Fox was wide awake in one second. She sat up, quivering all over. "Are you sure that's it?" she whispered.

"I'm positive! Listen!"

"They'll kill my children!" cried Mrs. Fox.

"Never!" said Mr. Fox.

"But darling, they will!" sobbed Mrs. Fox. "You know they will!"

Scrunch, scrunch, scrunch went the shovels above their heads. Small stones and bits of earth began falling from the roof of the tunnel.

"How will they kill us, Mummy?" asked one of the Small Foxes. His round black eyes were huge with fright. "Will there be dogs?" he said.

Mrs. Fox began to cry. She gathered her four children close to her and held them tight.

Suddenly there was an especially loud crunch above their heads and the sharp end of a shovel came right through the ceiling. The sight of this awful thing seemed to have an electric effect upon Mr. Fox. He jumped up and shouted, "I've got it! Come on! There's not a moment to lose! Why didn't I think of it before!"

"Think of what, Dad?"

"A fox can dig quicker than a man!" shouted Mr. Fox, beginning to dig. "Nobody in the world can dig as quick as a fox!"

The soil began to fly out furiously behind Mr. Fox as he started to dig for dear life with his front feet. Mrs. Fox ran forward to help him. So did the four children.

"Go downwards!" ordered Mr. Fox. "We've got to go deep! As deep as we possibly can!"

The tunnel began to grow longer and longer. It sloped steeply downward. Deeper and deeper below the surface of the ground it went. The mother and the father and all four of the children were digging together. Their front legs were moving so fast you couldn't see them. And gradually the scrunching and scraping of the shovels became fainter and fainter."

The foxes are *not* going to be killed by three nasty farmers! They dig with all their might to escape the men and their shovels. Draw the Fox family frantically digging deeper and deeper into the ground.

Caterpillar Tractors

"Bean rubbed the back of his neck with a dirty finger. He had a boil coming there and it itched. "What we need on this job," he said, "is machines . . . *mechanical* shovels. We'll have him out in five minutes with *mechanical s*hovels."

This was a pretty good idea, and the other two had to admit it.

✳ ✳ ✳

Soon, two enormous Caterpillar tractors with mechanical shovels on their front ends came clanking into the wood. Bean was driving one. Bunce the other. The machines were both black. They were murderous, brutal-looking monsters.

"Here we go, then!" shouted Bean.

"Death to the fox!" shouted Bunce.

The machines went to work, biting huge mouthfuls of soil out of the hill. The big tree under which Mr. Fox had dug his hole in the first place was toppled like a matchstick. On all sides, rocks were sent flying and trees were falling and the noise was deafening. "

These tractors mean serious business—within minutes, most of the hill has been eaten away. Draw the two enormous tractors with their mechanical shovels digging away at the earth on the hill.

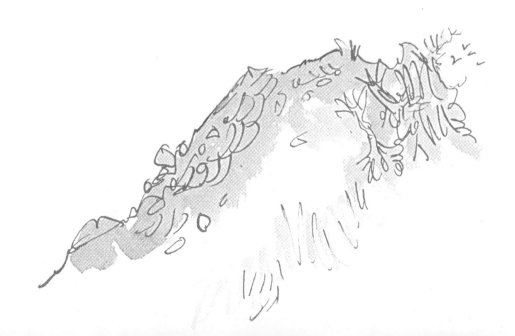

A FOX AMONG THE CHICKENS

"This time we must go in a very special direction," said Mr. Fox, pointing sideways and downward.

So he and his four children started to dig once again. The work went much more slowly now. Yet they kept at it with great courage, and little by little the tunnel began to grow.

"Dad, I wish you would tell us *where* we are going," said one of the children.

"I dare not do that," said Mr. Fox, "because this place I am *hoping* to get to is so *marvelous* that if I described it to you now you would go crazy with excitement. And then, if we failed to get there (which is very possible), you would die of disappointment. I don't want to raise your hopes too much, my darlings."

For a long long time they kept on digging. For how long they did not know, because there were no days and no nights down there in the murky tunnel. But at last Mr. Fox gave the order to stop. "I think," he said, "we had better take a peep upstairs now and see where we are. I know where I *want* to be, but I can't possibly be sure we're anywhere near it."

Slowly, wearily, the foxes began to slope the tunnel up towards the surface. Up and up it went . . . until suddenly they came to something hard above their heads and they couldn't go up any further. Mr. Fox reached up to examine this hard thing.

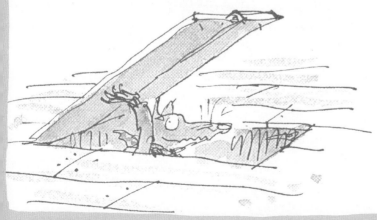

"It's wood!" he whispered. "Wooden planks!"

"What does that mean, Dad?"

"It means, unless I am very much mistaken, that we are right underneath somebody's house," whispered Mr. Fox. "Be very quiet now while I take a peek."

Carefully, Mr. Fox began pushing up one of the floorboards. The board creaked most terribly and they all ducked down, waiting for something awful to happen. Nothing did. So Mr. Fox pushed up a second board. And then, very very cautiously, he poked his head up through the gap. He let out a shriek of excitement.

"I've done it!" he yelled. "I've done it first time! I've done it! I've done it!"

He pulled himself up through the gap in the floor and started prancing and dancing with joy. "Come on up!" he sang out. "Come up and see where you are, my darlings! What a sight for a hungry fox! Hallelujah! Hooray! Hooray!"

The four Small Foxes scrambled up out of the tunnel and what a fantastic sight it was that now met their eyes! They were in a huge shed and the whole place was teeming with chickens. There were white chickens and brown chickens and black chickens by the thousand!

"Boggis's Chicken House Number One!" cried Mr. Fox. "It's exactly what I was aiming at! I hit it slap in the middle! First time! Isn't that fantastic! *And*, if I may say so, rather clever!"

The Small Foxes went wild with excitement. They started running around in all directions, chasing the stupid chickens. **"**

Mr. Fox and his family will not starve, after all! Chickens, chickens everywhere! Draw Mr. Fox dancing for joy among the chickens while the chickens fly around him.

The Cider Jar

"The Smallest Fox leaped high in the air. "Oh, Dad!" he cried out. "Look what we've found! It's cider!"

* * *

While they were talking, the Smallest Fox had sneaked a jar off the shelf and had taken a gulp. "Wow!" he gasped. "Wow-*ee*!"

You must understand this was not the ordinary weak fizzy cider one buys in a store. It was the real stuff, a home-brewed fiery liquor that burned in your throat and boiled in your stomach.

"Ah-h-h-h-h-h!" gasped the Smallest Fox. "This is *some cider*! "

The jar of cider is nearly bigger than the Smallest Fox! Draw the giant jar of cider that the Smallest Fox is drinking from.

A MOMENTOUS FEAST

"They grabbed their jars of cider and off they went. Mr. Fox was in front, the Smallest Fox came next, and Badger last. Along the tunnel they flew . . . past the turning that led to Bunce's Mighty Storehouse . . . past Boggis's Chicken House Number One and then up the long home stretch towards the place where they knew Mrs. Fox would be waiting.

"Keep it up, my darlings!" shouted Mr. Fox. "We'll soon be there! Think what's waiting for us at the other end! And just think what we're bringing home with us in these jars! That ought to cheer up poor Mrs. Fox." Mr. Fox sang a little song as he ran:

"Home again swiftly I glide,
Back to my beautiful bride.
She'll not feel so rotten
As soon as she's gotten
Some cider inside her inside."

Then Badger joined in:

"Oh poor Mrs. Badger, he cried,
So hungry she very near died.
But she'll not feel so hollow
If only she'll swallow
Some cider inside her
inside."

They were still singing as they rounded the final corner and burst in upon the most wonderful and amazing sight any of them had ever seen. The feast was just beginning. A large dining-room had been hollowed out of the earth, and in the middle of it, seated around a huge table, were no less than twenty-nine animals. They were:

Mrs. Fox and three Small Foxes.
Mrs. Badger and three Small Badgers.
Mole and Mrs. Mole and four Small Moles.
Rabbit and Mrs. Rabbit and five Small Rabbits.
Weasel and Mrs. Weasel and six Small Weasels.

The table was covered with chickens and ducks and geese and hams and bacon, and everyone was tucking into the lovely food.

"My darling!" cried Mrs. Fox, jumping up and hugging Mr. Fox. "We couldn't wait! Please forgive us!" Then she hugged the Smallest Fox of all, and Mrs. Badger hugged Badger, and everyone hugged everyone else. Amid shouts of joy, the great jars of cider were placed upon the table, and Mr. Fox and Badger and the Smallest Fox sat down with the others.

You must remember no one had eaten a thing for several days. They were ravenous. So for a while there was no conversation at all. There was only the sound of crunching and chewing as the animals attacked the succulent food. "

What a feast! After days running away and not eating, the underground animals are starved half to death. But what a feast they will enjoy!

Draw all the delicious food on the dinner table, and all the other animals happily sitting around it.

The Foxes' New Home

"There was a buzz of excitement around the table.

"I therefore invite you all," Mr. Fox went on, "to stay here with me for ever."

"For ever!" they cried. "My goodness! How marvelous!" and Rabbit said to Mrs. Rabbit, "My dear, just think! We're never going to be shot at again in our lives!"

"We will make," said Mr. Fox, "a little underground village, with streets and houses on each side–separate houses for Badgers and Moles and Rabbits and Weasels and Foxes. And every day I will go shopping for you all. And every day we will eat like kings."

The cheering that followed this speech went on for many minutes. "

None of the animals will ever need to go above ground again!
Draw the new underground village in the space below.

GEORGE'S GRANDMA

"George couldn't help disliking Grandma. She was a selfish grumpy old woman. She had pale brown teeth and a small puckered-up mouth like a dog's bottom.

"How much sugar in your tea today, Grandma?" George asked her.

"One spoonful," she said. "And no milk."

Most grandmothers are lovely, kind, helpful old ladies, but not this one. She spent all day and every day sitting in her chair by the window, and she was always complaining, grousing, grouching, grumbling, griping about something or other.

✳ ✳ ✳

When George's mother or father was home, Grandma never ordered George about like this. It was only when she had him on her own that she began treating him badly.

"You know what's the matter with you?" the old woman said, staring at George over the rim of the teacup with those bright wicked little eyes. "You're *growing* too fast. Boys who grow too fast become stupid and lazy."

"But I can't help it if I'm growing fast, Grandma," George said.

"Of course you can," she snapped. "Growing's a nasty childish habit."

"But we *have* to grow, Grandma. If we didn't grow, we'd never be grown-ups."

"Rubbish, boy, rubbish," she said. "Look at me. Am I growing? Certainly not."

"But you did once, Grandma."

"Only *very little*," the old woman answered.

"I gave up growing when I was extremely small, along with all the other nasty childish habits like laziness and disobedience and greed and sloppiness and untidiness and stupidity. You haven't given up any of these things, have you?"

"I'm still only a little boy, Grandma."

"You're eight years old," she snorted. "That's old enough to know better. If you don't stop growing soon, it'll be too late."

"Too late for what, Grandma?"

"It's ridiculous," she went on. "You're nearly as tall as me already."

George took a good look at Grandma. She certainly was a *very tiny* person. Her legs were so short she had to have a footstool to put her feet on, and her head only came halfway up the back of the armchair. "

What a nasty old woman George's grandma is! Draw her sitting all hunched-up in her chair, and George bringing her some tea.

The Cook-Up

"In the kitchen, George put the heavy stewing pot on the stove and turned up the gas flame underneath it as high as it would go.

Soon the marvelous mixture began to froth and foam. A rich blue smoke, the color of peacocks, rose from the surface of the liquid, and a fiery fearsome smell filled the kitchen. It made George choke and splutter. It was a smell unlike any he had smelled before. It was a brutal and bewitching smell, spicy and staggering, fierce and frenzied, full of wizardry and magic. Whenever he got a whiff of it up his nose, firecrackers went off in his skull and electric prickles ran along the backs of his legs. It was wonderful to stand there stirring this amazing mixture and to watch it smoking blue and bubbling and frothing and foaming as though it were alive. At one point, he could have sworn he saw bright sparks flashing in the swirling foam."

It looks like George has something marvelous brewing. Draw the pot bubbling and frothing and foaming, and the rich blue smoke and all the bright sparks flashing.

THE MARVELOUS INGREDIENTS

"George had absolutely no doubts whatsoever about how he was going to make his famous medicine. He wasn't going to fool about wondering whether to put in a little bit of this or a little bit of that. Quite simply, he was going to put in EVERYTHING he could find.

* * *

George decided to work his way around the various rooms one at a time and see what they had to offer.

He would go first to the bathroom . . .

GOLDENGLOSS HAIR SHAMPOO

TOOTHPASTE

SUPERFOAM SHAVING SOAP

VITAMIN ENRICHED FACE CREAM

NAIL POLISH

HAIR REMOVER

DISHWORTH'S FAMOUS DANDRUFF CURE

BRILLIDENT FOR CLEANING FALSE TEETH

NEVERMORE PONGING DEODORANT SPRAY

LIQUID PARAFFIN

* * *

. . . into the laundry room . . .

SUPERWHITE FOR AUTOMATIC
WASHING MACHINES

WAXWELL FLOOR POLISH

FLEA POWDER FOR DOGS

CANARY SEED

BROWN SHOE POLISH

. . . his mother's dressing table in the bedroom . . .

HELGA'S HAIRSET

FLOWERS OF TURNIPS

PINK PLASTER

LIPSTICKS

. . . to the kitchen . . .

GIN

A TIN OF CURRY POWDER

A TIN OF MUSTARD POWDER

A BOTTLE OF "EXTRA HOT" CHILI SAUCE

A TIN OF BLACK PEPPERCORNS

A BOTTLE OF HORSERADISH SAUCE

* * *

. . . the dusty old shed . . .

AN ORANGE-COLORED POWDER

ABOUT FIVE HUNDRED GIGANTIC PURPLE
PILLS

A BOTTLE OF THICK YELLOWISH LIQUID

A BRILLIANT RED LIQUID

PALE GREEN PILLS

. . . the garage . . .

ENGINE OIL

ANTIFREEZE

GREASE "

That sure is a long list of ingredients that George has found in his house—
this should fix Grandma up. Draw each of the ingredients that George has
found, from the Goldengloss Hair Shampoo to a whole tin of mustard powder.

Grandma through the Roof

"George stood in the farmyard looking up at the roof. The old farmhouse had a fine roof of pale red tiles and tall chimneys.

There was no sign of Grandma. There was only a song thrush sitting on one of the chimney pots, singing a song. The old wurzel's got stuck in the attic, George thought. Thank goodness for that.

Suddenly a tile came clattering down from the roof and fell into the yard. The thrush took off fast and flew away.

Then another tile came down.

Then half a dozen more.

And then, very slowly, like some weird monster rising up from the deep, Grandma's head came through the roof . . .

Then her scrawny neck . . .

And the tops of her shoulders . . .

"How'm I doing, boy!" she shouted. "How's that for a bash up?"

Oh dear. This is not *quite* what George was expecting. What will his parents say? Draw the very tall, skinny old woman poking out the top of the house.

THE FARM ANIMALS

"A second later, George's father appeared. His name was Mr. Killy Kranky. Mr. Kranky was a small man with bandy legs and a huge head. He was a kind father to George, but he was not an easy person to live with because even the smallest things got him all worked up and excited. The hen standing in the yard was certainly not a small thing, and when Mr. Kranky saw it, he started jumping about as though something was burning his feet. "Great heavens!" he cried, waving his arms.

"What's this? What's happened? Where did it come from? It's a giant hen! Who did it?"

"I did," George said.

"Look at *me*!" Grandma shouted from the rooftop. "Never mind about the hen! What about *me*?"

Mr. Kranky looked up and saw Grandma. "Shut up, Grandma," he said. It didn't seem to surprise him that the old girl was sticking up through the roof. It was the hen that excited him. He had never seen anything like it. But then who had?

"It's fantastic!" Mr. Kranky shouted, dancing around and around. "It's colossal! It's gigantic! It's tremendous! It's a miracle! How did you do it, George?"

George started telling his father about the magic medicine.

While he was doing this, the big brown hen sat down in the middle of the yard and went *cluck-cluck-cluck . . . cluck-cluck-cluck-cluck-cluck*.

Everyone stared at it.

When it stood up again, there was a brown egg lying there. The egg was the size of a football.

"That egg would make scrambled eggs for twenty people!" Mrs. Kranky said.

"George!" Mr. Kranky shouted. "How much of this medicine have you got?"

"Lots," George said. "There's a big potful in the kitchen, and this bottle here's nearly full."

"Come with me!" Mr. Kranky yelled, grabbing George by the arm. "Bring the medicine! For years and years I've been trying to breed bigger and bigger animals. Bigger bulls for beef. Bigger pigs for pork. Bigger sheep for mutton . . ."

They went to the pigsty first.

George gave a spoonful of the medicine to the pig.

The pig blew smoke from its nose and jumped about all over the place. Then it grew and grew.

In the end it looked like this . . .

They went to the herd of fine black bullocks that Mr. Kranky was trying to fatten for the market.

George gave each of them some medicine, and this is what happened . . .

Then the sheep . . .

He gave some to his gray pony, Jack Frost . . .

And finally, just for fun, he gave some to Alma, the nanny goat . . ."

George is now living on a farm full of colossal animals! Draw the gigantic pig, bullocks, sheep, gray pony, and nanny goat.

"**H**ere it is!" cried Mr. Killy Kranky, rushing into the kitchen. "One carton of flea powder for dogs and one can of brown shoe polish!"

George poured the flea powder into the giant stewing pot. Then he scooped the shoe polish out of its can and added that as well.

"Stir it up, George!" shouted Mr. Kranky. "Give it another boil! We've got it this time! I'll bet we've got it."

After Marvelous Medicine Number Three had been boiled and stirred, George took a cupful of it out into the yard to try it on another chicken. Mr. Kranky ran after him, flapping his arms and hopping with excitement.

"Come and watch this one!" he called out to Mrs. Kranky. "Come and watch us turning an ordinary chicken into a lovely great big one that lays eggs as large as footballs! "

Mr. Kranky has gone wild! He can't wait to make batches and batches more of George's marvelous medicine. Draw Mr. Kranky jumping around with excitement.